MAY 3 0 2013

W9-AQB-089

WITHDRAWN

by **Edith Hope Fine** and **Angela Demos Halpin**

Illustrated by **Colleen Madden**

TRICYCLE PRESS
Berkeley

THE KIDS IN ROOM 9 at Pepper Lane Elementary were tending their plants when Miss Marigold, the garden lady, dashed in.

"Look how your seeds have grown!" she said.

"All but mine," sighed Zack. "My radish croaked. Dead, dead, dead."

"Why?" she asked.

"I don't know. I watered it every single day," said Zack.

Miss Marigold raised her eyebrows.

"Oh," said Zack. "Too much?"

"That's okay." Miss Marigold pulled a seed packet from her hat. "Here, try again."

"My sunflower needs a home," said Daisy.

"Great idea. We could plant a garden," said Miss Marigold, as the recess bell rang. "Let's go find a spot."

Outside, the children looked for a garden home.

"Mr. Barks-a-Lot lives there," whispered Ben.
"I *know* things could grow by his yard."

"Mr. Barks-a-Lot?" asked Miss Marigold.

"Umm . . . we just call him that," said Ben.
"Mr. Barkley yells when we're too loud—or when
a ball hits his fence."

Zack stared at the weeds and litter. "Here? You're kidding."
"It's hard as a rock," said Daisy, scuffing the soil.
"Lots of gardens start out like this," said Miss Marigold.
Ben pushed aside prickly bushes. "Take a look!" he said.

The students took turns peeking through a knothole.
"Whoa!" said Daisy.
"No way!" said Zack.
"Fan-tastic," said Miss Marigold.

After recess, the students went back to the classroom full of ideas for their garden.

"But how do we start?" asked Zack.

"School gardens take plans, plants, and people," said Miss Marigold. "Then you water, weed, and wait."

ALL ABOUT A FLOWER

Ben remembered the messy weeds and trash. "We'll have to clean up first."

THAT SATURDAY, the Pepper Lane playground buzzed with activity. Teachers and students, moms and dads, neighbors and friends all worked together.

Mrs. Wheeler from the nursery handed out rakes and shovels. Mr. Flores from the hardware store brought pruners. Mr. Pappas the grocer served lemonade and oatmeal cookies.

Everyone trimmed and dug and raked and weeded.

"What's all that noise?" came a growly voice from behind the fence.
Up popped a big straw hat shading two grumpy eyebrows.

No one said a word. Zack backed away. Daisy hid behind a wheelbarrow.

"What's going on?" came the voice.

"It's Mr. Barks-a-Lot," Ben whispered.

"Who will explain to Mr. Barkley?" asked Miss Marigold, looking right at Ben.

Ben fidgeted with his shovel, then stepped forward.

"Hi, Mr. Barkley. We—we're the Pepper Lane cleanup crew."

"It's Saturday!" barked Mr. Barkley. "Shouldn't you all be home?"

"We're starting a garden—like yours." Ben pointed to the knothole.

"Hmmph," growled Mr. Barkley. He glared at all the sweaty workers.

Then he was gone.

Just as everyone was getting back to work, Mr. Barkley appeared on the Pepper Lane side of the fence.

"What are you staring at? We've got a lot to do!" he snapped.

Soon Miss Marigold and Mr. Barkley were huddled together, drawing plans in the dirt.

THE NEXT WEEK brought big changes—winding paths, a big yellow tub for watering, and a compost bin. Saws hummed and hammers banged to make garden boxes. Zack's dad backed a big truck onto the playground and dropped the tailgate. Out poured mounds of good rich soil.

AT LAST, planting day came.

"Meet my good guys for the garden," said Miss Marigold, holding up a bag.

"Ladybugs!" said Daisy.

"Right! They'll get to work when our work is done," said Miss Marigold. "Ready? Set? Dig!"

Everyone dug. Then they shook out seeds and planted veggies and flowers. Ladybugs flew into their new home.

As Ben smoothed dirt around a tomato plant, Mr. Barkley came over.

"Keep going," huffed Mr. Barkley. "Dig a shallow circle around the roots so the water seeps deep."

"Thanks," replied Ben.

"Hmmph," said Mr. Barkley.

A FEW DAYS LATER, Daisy discovered specks of green.

"Radishes!" she said.

"All they needed was soil, sun, and water," said Miss Marigold.

"But not *too* much water," said Zack.

EVERY WEEK the students gardened.

They watered.
They weeded.
They waited.

BIT BY BIT, all around the garden, peppers and zucchini, snow peas and bean vines, snapdragons and zinnias grew bigger and bigger.

ON ONE VISIT, Miss Marigold helped the class make a worm bin.

"Wiggly worms keep the soil loose," she said, reaching for a jar. "And now for some worm tea!"

"Worm tea?! Eeeew," said Zack.

"Not for you! For your plants," said Miss Marigold. "Worm poop is fabulous. Plants love it. Pests hate it."

SOON the garden brimmed with flowers and fruits and vegetables.
"Look what your hard work has done," said Miss Marigold. "Time to celebrate!"

THAT FRIDAY, the students dressed in garden costumes. When Daisy twirled, her pink petals swirled. Ben wriggled in his earthworm suit. Zack was a round red radish.

Fresh-picked flowers and garden treats covered the tables. There were enough fruit and veggie kebobs for everyone.

Ben heard humming from across the garden path.
Miss Marigold was escorted by a dancing carrot.
"Who *is* that?" Daisy asked.

The carrot bellowed a song for all to hear:
"Pepper Lane's the place to be.
Tomato slices, sweet mint tea,
Peppers, carrots, beans, and peas,
Cucumbers and strawberries,
Garden treats for you and me.
Pass the dips and yogurt, please!"

Everyone clapped. The singing carrot took a bow. Off flopped his green top.

"Mr. Barkley!" shouted Ben.

"Surprise!" said Mr. Barkley. "And I have another surprise."

He showed them dry brown pods that were frizzled at the top.

"Dead, dead, dead," said Zack.

"Not so fast," said Mr. Barkley, pulling at the pods.

"Seeds!" said Daisy. "What kind are they?"
"Who's your garden lady?" asked Mr. Barkley.
"Marigolds!" shouted the kids.
"Let's get planting," said Miss Marigold. "Then we'll . . .

water, weed,

. . . and wait!"

Sprouting Your Own School Garden

Tomatoes, strawberries, and squash fresh from the garden. What better way to introduce kids to gardening and healthful foods?

Across the country, school and community gardens open new worlds to children: from learning about the environment to sharing food with others, from promoting health and nutrition to having outdoor fun. Start by planting herbs, fruits, and vegetables that grow well where you live. Not sure how? Go to your local nursery or consult a Master Gardener. These knowledgeable volunteers can offer advice and support to help students start their own school gardens.

Online Resources

Miss Marigold says, "Take your questions to the Internet." You'll find information about grant money, garden pests, vermiculture and worm tea, and much more at these sites:

www.waterweedwait.com

www.mastergardenerssandiego.org

http://aggie-horticulture.tamu.edu/kindergarden/kinder.htm

http://www.csgn.org/

Checklist for a school garden

☐ **GET STARTED** Do research, plan your approach, gather resources (stories of successful gardens, state standards, and cost estimates), and get approval.

☐ **ORGANIZE** Build a team for garden planning, funding, and supplies: Master Gardeners, volunteers, teachers and staff, and local business owners can all help.

☐ **GO!** Select a site in full sun, clean it up, design your space, build garden beds, and celebrate planting day!

☐ **LEARN** Keep a journal: measure, sketch, and photograph your plants; study the critters in your garden; make notes on the weather and seasons; create stepping-stones and artwork.

☐ **KEEP GROWING!** Water, weed, feed, plant and replant . . . a gardener's job is never done! Change plantings with the seasons, evaluate progress, maintain funding and support.

☐ **TASTE** Eating and cooking your own plants is a fun part of gardening.

Now you're ready. Dig in and get those fingers dirty!

Garden Sketch To Do List
☐ Border/Frame ☐ design
☐ Date, Time, Weather
☐ SMArT = Art and Science
☐ Title: Garden, Flowers, Leaves, Petals, Color, or Texture
☐ Your name
LOOK and Draw

Leaves

Marilyn
U.C. Master Gardener
San Diego County

To our own favorite gardeners:
Chase, Taylor, Connor, and Jared –E.H.F.
William, Nicholas, and Dillon –A.D.H.

To P, S, & G . . . my mulching men! –C.M.

Text copyright © 2010 by Edith Hope Fine
and Angela Demos Halpin
Illustrations copyright © 2010 by
Colleen Madden

All photos on the school garden notes pages
by Marilyn Wieland, except the photo of
Marilyn, which was taken by Sharyn Fisky.

Library of Congress Cataloging-in-
Publication Data

Fine, Edith Hope.
    Water, weed, and wait / by Edith Hope Fine
and Angela Demos Halpin ; illustrations by
Colleen Madden.
        p. cm.
    1. Gardening—Juvenile literature. I. Halpin,
Angela Demos. II. Madden, Colleen M. III.
Title.
    SB457.F56 2010
    635—dc22
            2009032292

ISBN 978-1-58246-320-9 (hardcover)
ISBN 978-1-58246-355-1 (Gibraltar lib. bdg.)

Printed in China

Design by Katy Brown
Typeset in Proforma
The illustrations in this book were rendered
in mixed media.

1 2 3 4 5 6 – 14 13 12 11 10

First Edition

BT 5/30/13